RUN - JUMP - THROW
TRACK AND FIELD

Written and Illustrated by

George and Lynda Stuart

the Peppertree Press LLC

Sarasota, Florida

For information regarding permission,
call 941-922-2662 or contact us at our website:
www.peppertreepublishing.com or write to:
the Peppertree Press, LLC.
Attention: Publisher
1269 First Street, Suite 7
Sarasota, Florida 34236

ISBN: 978-1-61493-774-6

Library of Congress Number: 2021908413

Printed May 2021

Keep track of your numbers!

Color as you go, go, go!

One, one, I can run.

Two, two, I lost my shoe.

Three, three, I hurt my knee.

Four, four, may I please have more?

Five, five, see me dive!

Six, six, I found six sticks.

Seven, seven, it's half past eleven.

Eight, eight, he broke a plate.

Nine, nine, hanging on the clothes line.

Ten, ten, don't touch your chin.

Eleven, eleven, my sister is seven.

Twelve, twelve, behave yourself!

Thirteen, thirteen, stand in between.

Fourteen, fourteen, Jack could eat no lean.

Fifteen, fifteen, eat a jelly bean.

Sixteen, sixteen, my hat is green.

Seventeen, seventeen, don't be mean.

Eighteen, eighteen, see the moon beam.

Nineteen, nineteen, it's almost Halloween.

Twenty, twenty, I have plenty.

One, one, I can run.

Two, two, I lost my shoe.

3

Three, three, I hurt my knee.

Four, four, may I please have more?

5

Five, five, see me dive!

6

Six, six, I found six sticks.

Seven, seven, it's half past eleven.

Eight, eight, he broke a plate.

Nine, nine, hanging on the clothes line.

Ten, ten, don't touch your chin.

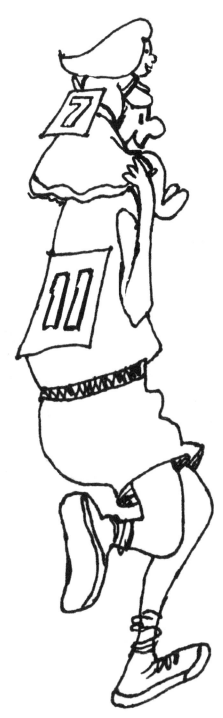

Eleven, eleven, my sister is seven.

Twelve, twelve, behave yourself!

Thirteen, thirteen, stand in between.

Fourteen, fourteen,
Jack could eat no lean.

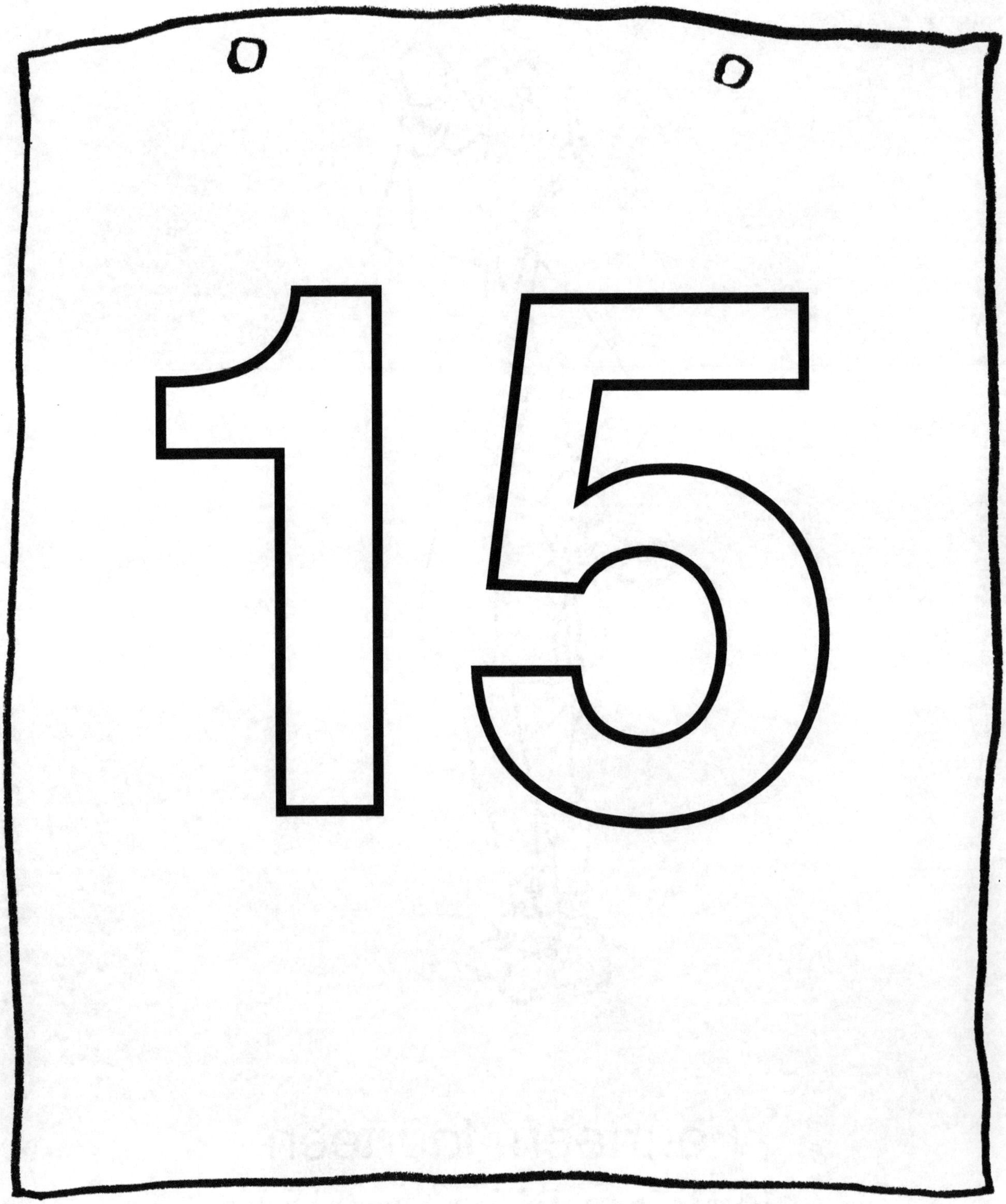
15

Fifteen, fifteen, eat a jelly bean.

Sixteen, sixteen, my hat is green.

(Can you color his hat green?)

Seventeen, seventeen, don't be mean.

Eighteen, eighteen,
see the moon beam.

Eighteen, eighteen,
see the moon beam.

Nineteen, nineteen,
it's almost Halloween.

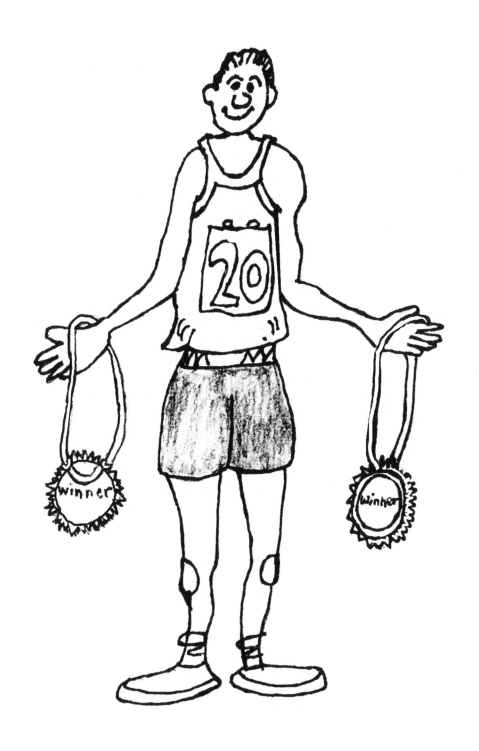

Twenty, twenty, I have plenty.

9 781614 937746